This Room is Mine!

Retold by Mary C. Olson
Illustrated by Gwen Connelly

Workbook Activities by Betty Glennon, B.S., M.S., Series Consultant

To the Parent

A love of books and good reading habits both begin at home -- from the picture books you shared with your child as a baby to the read-aloud stories he or she continues to enjoy.

Now your son or daughter is beginning to recognize words and read independently! Encouraging your child to read at home will help build confidence and enthusiasm for a skill he or she will use for a lifetime.

Here are some suggestions to help your beginning reader: Be sensitive to your child's abilities. Do not force your child, particularly if he or she is not yet learning to read in school.

- Be patient for 5 seconds so your child can try to sound out an unfamiliar word.

- Have your child skip an unknown word and read the rest of the sentence. Come back to the word and ask, "What word would make sense here?" Talk about it a little.

- Encourage your child to use any phonics skills that have been learned to help say the word, for example; beginning consonant sounds.

- Praise the effort!

- If a word is still unknown, say it for your child so he or she can continue reading.

- Encourage your child to use pictures as clues to words and meanings.

- Occasionally, before turning a page, ask your child to predict what will happen next. Praise his or her creative thinking.

- Help your child relate the story to his or her own experiences.

A GOLDEN® BOOK
Western Publishing Company, Inc.
Racine, Wisconsin 53404
No part of this book may be reproduced or copied in any form without written permission from the publisher. Produced in U.S.A.

"This room is mine!" said Dan. That was
what he said when he was mad at Bob.
"It is my room, too," said Bob.

"This is my bed," said Dan. He put his
hand on the bed. "This is my bat and my
car. This is my rug."

Dan got his fishing pole and put it down on the rug. Now the room had two sides.

"All of the things on this side of the pole are mine!" said Dan. "The bed is mine and the window is mine and the game box is mine and some of the closet is mine."

"Then, all of the things on this side are
mine," said Bob. "The desk is mine and the
lamp is mine and some of the closet is mine
and the door is mine."

Dan put his feet on one side of the pole.
Bob's feet were on his side. Their noses
almost hit.

"You can't have any of my air," said Dan.
"This is all my air over here!" said Bob.

Mother came to their door. "I just made
a cake," said Mother. "Who would like some?"
"I would!" Bob said. He ran out into the hall.

"I would, too," said Dan. He ran for the door, but then he saw the pole. The door was on Bob's side of the room.

"I don't want any cake," said Dan. He
went back and sat on his bed with his mitt
in his lap. When his mother came by
again, he was still there.

"You can go down and have some cake
with Bob," said Mother.

"I can't," Dan said. "This is my side of the room. Bob can't go on my side and I can't go on his."

Mother saw the pole. "Oh," she said.

"I will have to stay here and never go
out until I am an old, old man," said Dan.
"Well, I will come in to see you sometime,"
said Mother.

Dan would have to make plans if he had to stay on his side of the room until he was very, very old.

He would put his Christmas tree on the game box!

He would keep his car on the rug.

All of his pets would stay there with him and would not go over the pole.

When his friends came over, he would
pull them up in a basket.

Bob came in. His feet were on his side of the pole.

"I'm going to play ball with my friends," said Bob. "Do you want to come?"

"No," said Dan. "I'm going to stay here until I am an old, old man."

"You can be up first if you let us play with your bat," Bob said. "You can go out my door."

Dan was not mad now. It would be fun to play ball! The big boys did not let him play most of the time.

He saw the closet door. It made him think of something!

Dan got his bat. "I'll go down in the elevator,"
he said.

He went over to the closet and went inside.
"Going down!" he said.
"I want to ride in the elevator, too," said Bob.

Dan gave the door a tap so that it was on
Bob's side of the room.
"Get in," said Dan. "Going Down!"

"This stop for the ball game!" said Dan.
He put his fishing pole away.

"Hello," said Mother. "Do I see the boy who was going to stay in his room until he was very, very old?"

"My side of the room was too little, " said Dan. "I'm going to play ball with Bob's friends."

And he and Bob ran outside.